GREATEST MOMENTS

of the NBA

by Bruce Weber

SCHOLASTIC INC.

New York   Toronto   London   Auckland   Sydney
Mexico City   New Delhi   Hong Kong

To a truly great moment:
March 3, 1998 — the arrival of
my main man, Max P. Kraemer.

PHOTO CREDITS:
NBA Photos
Cover(Robinson/Duncan): Lou Cappozzola. **Cover(Chamberlain), 6, 9, 11:** NBA Photo Library.
Cover(Johnson), 20, 21, 22, 23, 24: Andrew D. Bernstein. **Cover(Pippen), 26, 30:** Nathaniel S. Butler.
3: Wen Roberts. **8:** Dick Raphael. **10:** George Kalinsky. **12, 14, 15:** Neil Leifer. **13, 16:** Walter Iooss, Jr.
18, 19: Bill Baptist. **28:** Fernando Medina. **29:** Gary Dineen.

ISBN 0-439-14072-2

© 2000 by NBA Properties, Inc.
All rights reserved. Published by Scholastic Inc.

12 11 10 9 8 7 6 5 4 3 2 1   0 1 2 3 4 5 6/0

Printed in the U.S.A.
First Scholastic printing, February 2000
Book design: Michael Malone

Momentous Occasions

If this were truly a book of the NBA's Greatest Moments, it might be thousands of pages long. In its more than 50-year history, the world's greatest basketball league has produced thousands of memorable accomplishments and performances. But in order to save zillions of trees, we've boiled down the list to only the most vital of those great moments.

What's a moment? The dictionary defines it as a particular time of significance. And every one of the greatest moments in this book qualifies as that. But while some moments only take an instant, some of them last a lot longer. There are moments in this book that involve a single play or a few minutes of action. But there are others that occupy a season and even a decade. The league's first game, which was followed by thousands more, is included too.

Certainly we left out dozens of amazing moments. In the 1973 NBA Finals, for example, the Lakers' Jerry West canned a 60-foot shot at the buzzer, tying the score against the Knicks to force overtime in Game 3. If there were three-point goals in those days, West's shot would have been the game winner.

You won't find Julius Erving's amazing playoff scoop shot from behind the backboard or Scott Skiles' incredible 30-assist game for the Orlando Magic against the Denver Nuggets in 1990. You won't learn about the Detroit Pistons' repeat NBA championships in 1989 and 1990.

But you will meet some of the greatest teams (the Celtics of the '60s, the Lakers of the '80s, and the Bulls of the '90s). You'll read about Julius "Dr. J" Erving, who was flying around NBA courts before Michael Jordan ever had a chance to try out for his high school basketball team. And you'll get a sense of some of the league's greatest rivalries—team versus team and player versus player.

The NBA produces great moments every game. The highlight videos you see on TV give you just one indication of how great today's players really are. Basketball is immensely physical. But it is also beautiful. The players move so smoothly, jump so effortlessly. They practically fly through the air.

Now take a look at the NBA when it was young. Relive the accomplishments of favorite players—Wilt the Stilt, Dr. J, Michael, Magic, Tim. You will be amazed.

WILLIS REED AND WILT CHAMBERLAIN

Opening Night

So you think the Toronto Raptors and the Vancouver Grizzlies are the NBA's first teams in Canada? No way. The Toronto Huskies were the league's first Canadian team. And they hosted the NBA's very first game—against the New York Knicks.

The date was November 1, 1946. It was nothing like today's NBA. In fact, the league was called the BAA—the Basketball Association of America. There was no shot clock. Most of the players were relatively short, fairly slow, and anchored to the floor. Coaches didn't believe players could shoot as well in the air as they could with both feet on the floor.

The BAA was organized only five months before the first game. There had been other leagues before, though never very organized. This new league was going to be different. Most of the BAA's team owners also owned the arenas. They needed to put events into their buildings. Many already owned National Hockey League teams but knew little about basketball. That didn't stop them from creating the BAA.

They changed the rules a little to make professional games different from college games. College games were 40 minutes long and played in two halves; pro games were 48 minutes long and played in four quarters. Zone defenses were out because they slowed down the game. And there was one other major difference: Players were paid about $5,000 for the season, about what a superstar gets for one minute today!

Of course, lower player salaries made for lower ticket prices. For the league's first game, the highest-priced seat at Maple Leaf Gardens cost only $2.50. You could get in for as little as 75 cents. And if you were taller than the Huskies' tallest player, 6–8 George Nostrand, you got in free!

More than 7,000 fans showed up for the new league's opener. Most of them knew plenty about hockey, little about basketball. But, as the game got underway, they really got into it. The Knicks scored the first six points, led 16–12 at the end of the first quarter, and built their lead to 15 points in the second period. The Huskies rallied to trail by only eight at halftime and briefly led in the second half. But New York closed strongly and pulled out a 68–66 victory. The new league was on its way!

The Toronto Huskies never made it to the second season. Other teams came and went as the league grew. Two years later, the BAA merged with another league, the National Basketball League, and became the NBA. The rest, as they say, is history—glorious history!

The Magic Clock

When the 1953–54 season ended, the NBA was in trouble. The league's number one drawing card, Minneapolis' great center, George Mikan, had retired. Despite some rules that were designed to speed up games, coaches and players had found ways to get around them. The games were slow, boring and, thanks to lots of late-game fouls, unbearably long. If that continued, the league—and maybe even the game of basketball—could be in big, big trouble.

Enter Danny Biasone, who could possibly be the NBA's all-time superstar without ever scoring a single basket. Biasone was the owner of the Syracuse Nationals. He realized that a crisis was at hand. His team had lost to the Minneapolis Lakers in the 1954 Finals. But the scores were more like high school games. Syracuse had won at Minneapolis by 62–60 and 65–63. (Of course, neither of those contests compared to the all-time snorer: a 19–18 victory by Fort Wayne over Minneapolis in 1950. That time, the two teams combined for 13 points in the entire second half!)

So Biasone and his general manager, Leo Ferris, went to work on the problem. First they convinced the league to limit the number of fouls each team could commit in a quarter. After the first four fouls, extra foul shots would be awarded. That would cut down on the number of fouls.

But the pace of the game was even more important. Biasone figured a clock would do it. Teams couldn't be allowed to hold the ball forever. They would have to shoot within a certain period of time. Biasone watched a few films, played with a stopwatch at some games, and decided the proper amount of time would be 24 seconds. As it turned out, it was one of those magic numbers in sports. The distance between bases in baseball is 90 feet. It's perfect. The size of the goal in hockey is 4'x 6'. It's perfect.

So, as it turns out, was Danny Biasone's 24-second clock. Since 1954, NBA teams have been shooting within 24 seconds after taking possession of the ball. They don't have to rush, but they can't pass the ball around forever.

The results of the Biasone clock were immediate. Average per team scoring the year before the clock was 79.5 points per game. In the clock's first season, it was 93.1. That's exactly what Biasone and the NBA had in mind.

Today, most basketball games in the world operate with a shot clock. The times vary. In women's basketball, for instance, it's 30 seconds. In men's college basketball, it's 35 seconds. In international basketball, men and women use a 30-second clock. And every one of those clocks ows its existence to Danny Biasone.

WILT CHAMBERLAIN

Game of the Century

There were 4,124 fans at the Hershey Arena in Pennsylvania on March 2, 1962. Another 100,000 or so claim to have been there. All of them say they saw the greatest one-game performance in the history of the NBA. That was the night Wilton Norman Chamberlain of the Philadelphia Warriors scored 100 points.

At 7–1 and 275 pounds (at least), Chamberlain was the classic big man. He was amazing at both ends of the floor and a wonderful athlete. His rivalry with the Boston Celtics' superstar Bill Russell was the stuff of NBA legend. The mere sight of the other juiced each man up and made him play like crazy. In fact, one night in 1960, Chamberlain grabbed an amazing 55 rebounds (an NBA record that still stands) against the Celts.

This night in Hershey was extraordinary. The Knicks knew they were in trouble before the game began. Their starting center, Phil Jordon, was out with the flu. His backups, Darrall Imhoff and Cleveland Buckner, couldn't keep up with the man they called "Wilt the Stilt." And the Warriors knew it.

Chamberlain tossed down 23 points in the first quarter and, by halftime, he had 41. He had an excellent chance to break his NBA single-game scoring record. Wilt had scored 78 points in a game earlier that season.

He kept up the pace in the third quarter. His 28 points in that period gave him a total of 69. The record was well within reach. The fans knew they were seeing something special. "Give it to Wilt! Give it to Wilt!" they screamed.

The Warriors were listening. It took only a few minutes for Chamberlain to set a record, but no one was satisfied with that. The Warriors and the fans all wanted Wilt to score 100 points. The Knicks, of course, didn't see it that way. They fouled the other Warriors to prevent Wilt from scoring. But Philly was determined. In fact, with the game no longer in doubt, they fouled New York players to get the ball back.

Wilt hit 90 and kept right on going. Finally, with 46 seconds to go, he hit a short shot. Bang! 100 points! The fans raced out of the seats and onto the floor. Chamberlain took off for the locker room. The game ended early with a 169–147 Philly win. Wilt had hit 36 of 63 field goal attempts, huge numbers. But even more surprising was his free throw shooting. Wilt was known as one of the league's worst foul shooters, hitting barely half of his attempts. But on this night, he hit 28 of 32 tries.

He wound up the season averaging 50.4 points per game, becoming the only player in NBA history to score more than 4,000 points in a single season. Remarkable yes, but his 100-point night was absolutely mind boggling—and totally unforgettable!

At 7–1 and 275 pounds, Chamberlain was the classic big man.

BILL RUSSELL

8

One More Time for Red

The Decade of the Celtics wasn't exactly boring. The games were usually tight and exciting. Nevertheless, from 1959 to 1965, when they handed out championship rings, they always wound up on the fingers of the Boston Celtics and their legendary coach, Red Auerbach.

But 1966 looked to be the year of change. For the first time in a decade, Boston didn't win the Eastern Division. Philadelphia did. A future Hall of Famer named Billy Cunningham joined NBA scoring champ Wilt Chamberlain, Luke Jackson, Chet Walker and the rest of the Sixers' gang to unseat the Celts. In fact, they won their last 11 games to take the title by one game. Along the way, they beat Boston six times in 10 meetings. The world, as the NBA knew it, was about to change. Or was it?

He won't admit it, but Auerbach juiced up the Celtics by announcing his retirement as coach after the season. That was all Boston needed. After trailing the Cincinnati Royals two games to one in the best-of-five opening round of the playoffs, they rallied to win. Next was Philadelphia. The Sixers had enjoyed a two-week vacation while Boston battled Cincinnati. It was too long. Boston was barely tested as they upset the regular-season leaders, four games to one. The folks in Philly were so upset that the Sixers fired their coach, Dolph Schayes!

Meanwhile, the L.A. Lakers and St. Louis Hawks were locked in a death match out west. It went the full seven games before L.A. pulled it out. It was on to Boston.

Would the Lakers be too tired to end the Boston streak? It didn't seem like it when L.A. won the opener in overtime at Boston Garden. That's when Auerbach played his winning card. He announced that the Celtics' immortal center, Bill Russell, would succeed him as coach. That was all the players needed. With their old coach on the bench and their new coach doing amazing things on the floor, they ran off victories in the next three games.

With their backs against the wall, the Lakers rallied. They took Games 5 and 6, tying the series. It all came down to Game 7 at Boston Garden. Auerbach, Russell, and Co. were ready. They won a thriller, 95–93, giving Red the sendoff he wanted. It was the Celtics' eighth straight championship and their ninth in 10 years. The NBA's most dominant team had put together the greatest decade in the history of professional sports.

For the first time in a decade, Boston didn't win the Eastern Division.

WILLIS REED AND
WILT CHAMBERLAIN

The Limping Hero

Would you believe that a player can score only four points and still lead his team to victory? Well, it's true. Just ask anyone who saw the final game of the 1970 NBA Finals.

It was one of basketball's classic matchups: Game 7 between the New York Knicks and the Los Angeles Lakers on May 8, 1970. Lakers' fans will tell you that Game 7 never should have happened. The series was tied at two games apiece when Game 5 was played at New York's Madison Square Garden. Early on, with the Lakers comfortably ahead, the Knicks lost their captain and leader, Willis Reed. He had torn a muscle in his right thigh. He was through for the night and probably for the season. But the Knicks, somehow, rallied to win, taking a three games to two lead.

The Lakers easily captured Game 6 in L.A. Wilt Chamberlain, in his second year with L.A. after a long career with the Warriors and 76ers, led his team with 45 points and 27 rebounds. Without Reed, their fallen hero, the Knicks never had a chance.

That set up a deciding Game 7, back in New York. It would be a Lakers' blowout, said most of the experts. But they never expected a medical miracle named Willis Reed.

When the teams took the floor for pregame warm-ups, Reed was nowhere to be seen. He wasn't on the court and he wasn't on the bench. One minute before tipoff, the Knick captain came limping down the aisle leading from the locker room. Some fans spotted him and began cheering. Quickly every eye in the building turned to the 6–10, 240-pound superstar.

Could he play? He could hardly lift his right leg. When he ran, he dragged the injured leg behind him. But Willis was determined to play, determined to help his team win the championship, something no Knick team had ever done.

Amazingly, Reed challenged Chamberlain but lost the opening tip. In the Knicks first possession, they worked the ball to their captain who tossed in a 21-footer to give New York a 2–0 lead. The place went wild. The Lakers didn't believe what they were seeing. The next time up the court, New York found Reed open for another 20-footer. Swish! Two shots, four points. The roof practically came off the building.

Willis Reed would score no more that night, but his surprisingly active defense frustrated Chamberlain for most of the first half. He sat down at halftime and did not return. But his teammates were so uplifted it didn't matter. Walt Frazier went on to score 36 points and dish off 19 assists to lead New York. The Lakers were shell-shocked. The Knicks led by as many as 29 points in the first half, then coasted to an improbable 113–99 victory.

Willis Reed was voted MVP of both the 1969–70 season and the 1970 NBA Finals. But no honor was as great as the incredible four-point, one-legged effort that earned his Knicks their first NBA title!

> Quickly every eye in the building turned to the 6-10, 240-pound superstar.

JERRY WEST

The Streak

When the 1970–71 Milwaukee Bucks won an NBA-record 20 straight games, everyone thought the mark would last for a long time. The Bucks were led by young Kareem Abdul-Jabbar and went on to sweep the NBA Finals that year. This was one for the history books.

So it surprised no one that the Bucks were favored to repeat their win the following year. Though the L.A. Lakers were always a strong team, no one thought they'd be around to challenge the defending champs. Their big guns, Wilt Chamberlain, Jerry West and Elgin Baylor, were almost elderly by NBA standards. In fact, eight games into the season, Baylor's knees forced him to retire.

So coach Bill Sharman had to make some changes. He inserted Jim McMillian into Baylor's forward spot. Guard Gail Goodrich assumed more of the scoring load, while West continued to pour in points and run the offense. Chamberlain, ever the great rebounder, turned his attention on offense toward setting up his teammates. He and forward Happy Hairston dominated the boards. The changes seemed almost magical.

On November 5, the Lakers squeezed out a four-point victory over the Baltimore Bullets. The next time they lost, the calendar had already flipped to 1972!

Five weeks after the Baltimore victory, in mid-December, the Lakers beat Atlanta, 104–95. It was their 21st straight win, erasing Milwaukee's untouchable record. It had lasted less than one year! The L.A. streak continued.

On December 22, the Lakers passed another milestone. When they beat the Bullets (again!), it marked their 27th straight victory. Fifty-six years earlier, the 1916 New York Giants baseball team had won 26 games in a row. L.A. had now won more games in a row than any other professional sports team.

How long could it continue? On January 7, 1972, 63 nights after the first victory, the Lakers routed the Atlanta Hawks, 134–90, extending the streak to 33 straight. No other team in any professional sport had ever come close to that number. And no team ever has since.

Then, on January 9, it all ended at the hands of the old record-holders, the Bucks. The tired Lakers lost 120–104.

Coach Sharman, a superstar in his own right with the Celtics, took the streak in stride. "I knew it had to end sometime," he said in the locker room. "But my players and I would trade the streak for a championship ring any time."

The coach had nothing to worry about. With 33 wins in 33 games, the Lakers went on to a 69–13 season, the best record ever at that time. And they capped their remarkable 1971–72 season by beating the New York Knicks in five games in the NBA Finals.

> No one thought that L.A. would be around to challenge the defending champs.

NATE "TINY" ARCHIBALD

Tiny the Terror

Almost anywhere in the world, a 6–1 man is fairly big. Not so in the NBA. That's why 6–1 Hall of Famer Nate Archibald was called "Tiny." And the feat he accomplished in 1972–73, probably never to be equaled, was absolutely huge.

Tiny Archibald's story is both unlikely and amazing. Born in the poorest area of the Bronx, New York, young Nate was cut from his high school basketball team. That should have been the end of the story. And it could have been, had Tiny not taken full advantage of his lucky second chance. He went on to become an All-City high school player and then a college player on scholarship (Texas Western in El Paso).

By then, folks everywhere had begun to hear about Tiny Archibald. The Cincinnati Royals, coached by Hall of Famer Bob Cousy, picked him in the second round of the 1970 NBA Draft. His rookie year was so-so. His 16 points per game were offset by poor defense and ballhandling. Gradually, however, both improved. In the middle of his second season, he was left off the NBA All-Star team. That irked Archibald, so he raised his scoring to 34 points per game in the second half of the year.

That set the stage for his record-breaking 1972–73 season. The Royals packed up shop in Cincinnati and became a two-city team—the Kansas City/Omaha Kings. This was the year that Tiny became King!

He kept up the scoring pace, hitting 34 points per game. That was no surprise. Archibald had proved he could score in bunches. His amazing quickness enabled him to thread his way through the tall trees clogging the middle of the court. And he could pull up and drill the jumper when defenders sagged to keep him away from the basket.

The surprise was that Tiny also became the league's best floor manager. He dashed off 11.4 assists per game. Both totals led the NBA. No one before—or since—accomplished that double.

Folks everywhere had begun to hear about Tiny Archibald.

Injuries and off-court problems bothered Archibald in other seasons, though he did help lead the 1981 Boston Celtics to his only NBA title. When it was all over, after 14 pro seasons, Tiny had scored 16,481 points, dashed off 6,476 assists, and played in six All-Star Games. And, in 1991, he won the biggest honor of all, election to the Naismith Memorial Basketball Hall of Fame.

JOHN HAVLICEK

The Longest Game

It was a typical Boston Garden night on June 4. The old place was not air-conditioned. So with a full house on hand for Game 5 of the 1976 NBA Finals, the Garden was hot! The series matched the hometown Boston Celtics, the league's most dominant team, and the Phoenix Suns, an expansion team that had never won a title. After four games, it was all even.

Boston raced to a 20-point first-quarter lead, but Phoenix managed to chip away. The Suns cut their deficit to fifteen at halftime, and their defense shut down the Celtics in the second half. At the end of the regulation 48 minutes, the teams wound up tied, forcing overtime. That happened frequently. But if the fans thought they'd be heading home after another five minutes of action, they were seriously mistaken.

Still, the game almost ended in the first overtime. Boston's Paul Silas tried to call a timeout toward the end of the period. But the Celts were out of timeouts. It would have produced a technical foul that would have given Phoenix a chance to win. But referee Richie Powers didn't acknowledge Silas' signal and the game continued.

The second overtime was even better. Phoenix led by one with four seconds to go. But Boston's superstar, John Havlicek, charged down the floor and banked in a 15-footer to seemingly give the Celts a one-point victory. The fans, thinking the game was over, poured onto the famed Garden floor to celebrate. The scoreboard clock read :00. But the celebration came too soon. The officials ruled that one second remained.

They cleared the court and gave the ball to the Suns. But they were 94 feet away from their hoop. It would be impossible to score. A timeout would give Phoenix the ball at mid-court but, like Boston in the first overtime, they were out of timeouts. The penalty for calling an illegal timeout was a technical foul. Boston would get a free throw, possibly increasing their lead to two points. What would the Suns do?

The Suns' Paul Westphal didn't hesitate. He called the timeout any-way. Boston got the technical foul, made the free throw, and led by two. But that one second still remained on the clock and now, according to the rules, Phoenix would inbound from midcourt. The inbound pass went to Garfield Heard who turned and tossed in a 23-footer as the buzzer sounded. That tied the score. Incredibly, a third overtime began.

But that was Phoenix's last gasp. Glenn McDonald, a little-used reserve, came off the Boston bench to hit for six points in the third overtime. The Celtics survived to win 128–126. Both teams were exhausted. So were the fans.

Two days later, back in Phoenix, Boston won 87–80—in a standard 48 minutes—to take the title, four games to two. It was the Celtics' 13th NBA champi-onship. The Suns have yet to win their first. But Game 5, the only 63-minute game in Finals history, remains perhaps the greatest game ever!

With a full house on hand for

Game 5 of the 1976 NBA Finals,

the Garden was hot!

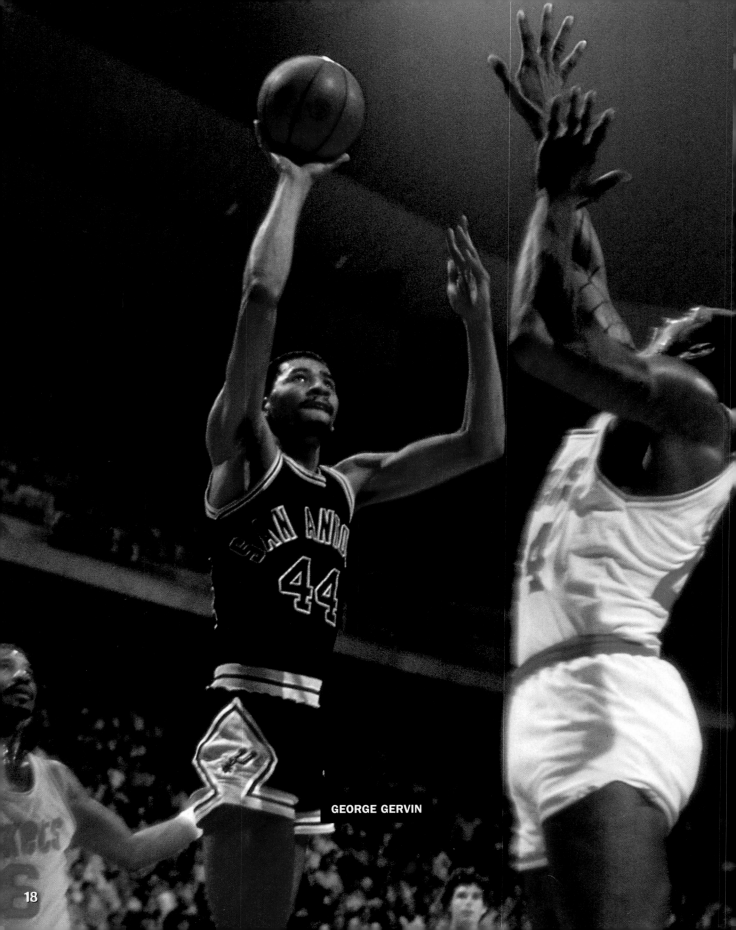

GEORGE GERVIN

The Iceman Scores

Never in NBA history did two players battle so hard for a scoring title. One day, Denver's David Thompson would take the lead. The next day, San Antonio's George Gervin would edge in front.

They were both destined to go to the Hall of Fame. Thompson had great physical tools. The 6–4½ superstar had led his North Carolina State team to the NCAA Championship in 1974. Now he was showing pro fans how he did it. Gervin, on the other hand, was smooth and cool. When the game was on the line, he wanted the ball. His fans called him "The Iceman" because he was so cool under pressure.

At the start of play on April 9, 1978, the final day of the 1977–78 season, Gervin led the scoring race with an average of 26.8 points per game. Thompson was right behind with 26.6.

The schedule worked out beautifully. David's Denver Nuggets faced the Detroit Pistons in an afternoon game. His teammates wanted him to win the title so they gave him the ball every chance they could.

Thompson scored 32 points in the first quarter, setting an NBA record. At halftime, he had 53. In the second half, his teammates kept feeding him. He wound up with 73 points, which equaled the third-highest single-game total in NBA history. Incredibly his scoring average soared to 27.15 points per game. Playing an exhausting 43 minutes, David hit on an amazing 28 of 38 shots from the field and 17 of 20 from the foul line.

So when the Spurs visited the New Orleans Jazz that night, Gervin—and his team-mates—knew what they had to do. If he wanted the scoring crown, he would have to score at least 58 points. It wouldn't be easy, but the Spurs were determined to get the title for their main man. They kept feeding him the ball and he kept shooting—and scoring.

Gervin scored 20 points in the first quarter, then dumped in 33 points in the second quarter, breaking Thompson's record, which had lasted for less than six hours! At half-time, he was up to 53. He needed only five more points.

They came quickly. When The Iceman scored six points early in the second half, sewing up the championship, he took a seat on the bench. He wound up with 63 points though he played 10 minutes less than Thompson. Gervin hit 23 of 49 from the field and 17 of 20 from the line.

When the dust settled, Gervin's scoring average was 27.22, a mere .07 of one point ahead of Thompson. Both of their teams won their division championships. Denver made it to the Conference Finals before losing to Seattle. San Antonio lost in the Conference Semifinals to the eventual NBA champion Washington Bullets. But the scoring battle between their Hall of Fame superstars is what Nuggets and Spurs fans remember most about the spring of 1978!

His fans called him "The Iceman" because he was so cool under pressure.

JULIUS ERVING

20

The Doctor Is In

From the moment Julius Erving arrived in pro basketball, everyone knew he was special. Fresh out of the University of Massachusetts in 1971, he joined the American Basketball Association's Virginia Squires and instantly averaged 27.3 points. After leading the league in scoring in 1972–73, Erving was traded to the ABA's New York Nets, and he led his new team to a league title. Then, in 1976, the NBA/ABA merger and a last-minute trade landed him with the Philadelphia 76ers. The Doctor, as everyone called him, was where he belonged—in basketball's best league.

In his new home, Dr. J continued to dazzle. No one in the game had his moves. The only thing he didn't have was an NBA championship ring. The Sixers came close several times, but they lacked a big man to complete their game.

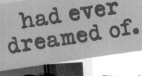

He had moves on the court that no one had ever dreamed of.

They got him before the 1982–83 season. Philly dealt center Caldwell Jones and a first-round draft pick to the Houston Rockets for Moses Malone, the NBA's Most Valuable Player. Malone gave the team a big body who could score (24.5 points per game in 1982–83) and rebound (15.3 per game, tops in the league). Moses took the pressure off the Doctor—and made the Sixers a championship team.

They romped through the regular season. Their 65–17 record was the league's best. But the playoffs marked a brand-new season. The Sixers never looked back. Before the first game, Malone made his prediction: "Fo', Fo', Fo'," meaning that Philly would beat each opponent in four straight. It was an outrageous pick. No team in history had ever done that. Moses' words were at the top of the bulletin board in every team's locker room.

But Coach Billy Cunningham and the Sixers were more than up to the task. With Dr. J and Malone in top form, it actually turned out to be fairly easy. The New York Knicks went down in four straight in the opening round. The Doctor was on call. And when the offense bogged down, the Sixers dumped the ball into Malone, who simply turned and scored.

In the Conference Finals, the Milwaukee Bucks modified Malone's prediction. They actually won a game. But Philly took the series, four games to one. Then in the NBA Finals, it was the Sixers over the Lakers in four straight.

The Doctor finally had his ring. It was the perfect cap to a great career. Erving had been Michael Jordan before there was a Michael Jordan. He had moves on the court that no one had ever dreamed of. People everywhere watched the Sixers play just to get a glimpse of their whirling, hang-in-the-air Doctor. And engraved on his only NBA championship ring was the corrected version of Moses Malone's prediction: "Fo', Five, Fo'."

LARRY BIRD AND
MAGIC JOHNSON

Magic's Moment

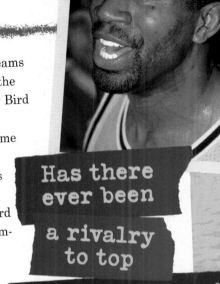

When you talk about great NBA rivalries, it's usually two great teams butting heads: the Knicks and the Bulls, the Celtics and the Sixers, the Bulls and the Pistons. But has there ever been a rivalry to top Larry Bird and Magic Johnson?

It began in their college days. The 1979 NCAA Championship Game matched Johnson of powerhouse Michigan State against Bird of unknown (but unbeaten) Indiana State. Everyone in the country was talking about it. Magic's team pulled out the victory and the rivalry was born. The following year, the first for each as a pro, Boston's Bird won NBA Rookie of the Year honors; L.A. and Johnson won the championship. And that was just the start of things.

The rivalry reached fever pitch when the two met in the NBA Finals for the first time in 1984. Bird's Celtics won in seven games and Larry was the series MVP. Round two to Bird. They were right back at it the following year. This time it was Magic's turn. The Lakers won in six games. Magic led 2–1.

Has there ever been a rivalry to top Larry Bird and Magic Johnson?

That was the scene as the two teams—and two superstars—met to decide the 1987 world title. The flashy, Showtime Lakers had gotten there rather easily, beating up on Denver, Golden State and Seattle while losing only once (to the Warriors) along the way. Boston had it a lot tougher, taking the full seven games to upend both the Milwaukee Bucks in the Eastern Conference Semifinals and the Detroit Pistons in the Eastern Conference Finals.

The tired Celts were simply not ready to challenge the Lakers in Game 1 on the West Coast. Magic came close to a triple-double with 29 points, 13 assists, and eight rebounds as L.A. won handily by 13. Could Boston crack down on the Lakers' star? Not really.

Johnson was even better in Game 2. His 22 points and 20 assists keyed the L.A. attack. Just as important, he set up Michael Cooper for six three-pointers. The result: a convincing 141–122 thrashing. The Lakers, who had won 65 regular-season games, were now just two wins from another league title.

Boston won Game 3 back in Boston Garden, making Game 4 critical for both teams. It was spectacular. Hardly anyone in the overheated Garden was sitting when Magic tossed in a running hook shot with a couple of seconds to go to give L.A. a gripping 107–106 victory.

That was about it. The Celtics kept the series going by winning Game 5 at home. But that was their last gasp. The Lakers went home to the Forum and put the finishing touches on their spectacular season. After a sluggish first half, L.A. outscored Boston 55–37 after intermission to run away with a 106–93 victory. When the media voted at game's end, Finals' MVP was strictly no contest. Magic Johnson had done it again!

1992 OLYMPIC TEAM

24

The Dream Team

Once upon a time, the United States owned basketball. The game was invented in the U. S., improved in the U. S., and perfected in the U. S. Though the sport was created in 1891, it wasn't until 1936 that it became an Olympic event. And then the U. S. showed the rest of the world how much catching up they had to do. It wasn't until 1972, in a controversial game against the Soviet Union, that the American team lost an Olympic basketball game.

By 1988, the U. S. domination began to fade. The reason: In other countries, the best players practiced and played together for years on national teams. The U.S. used college players who got together only a few weeks before the games. Even international teams and officials knew it was not fair to prevent NBA players from competing in the Olympics and other events and, in the spirit of the Olympic ideal, they wanted to compete against the best. So, led by an international movement, the rules were changed in 1989 to allow all players to compete in international events.

The U.S was able to use its best pros at the 1992 games. Imagine Larry Bird, Magic Johnson, Michael Jordan and the rest of the NBA superstars on one team. What a dream that would be! And so the first Dream Team was born.

Suddenly, there they were on the court in Barcelona. In addition to Michael and Magic and Larry, the rest of the cast was fabulous. The centers were David Robinson and Patrick Ewing. John Stockton, soon to be the NBA's all-time assist leader, played the point. His Jazz teammate Karl Malone was set at power forward. Outspoken Charles Barkley led a group that could play almost anywhere: Chris Mullin, Clyde Drexler and Scottie Pippen. Christian Laettner, the college player of the year, rounded out the squad.

Everywhere they went, they were mobbed. "It was like coaching a bunch of rock stars," said Coach Chuck Daly. Could this team lose? Sure, if the team bus got lost for a couple of hours. The opponents had no shot. But they didn't mind getting smashed. In fact, they posed for pictures with their rivals, just to show their grandkids that they played against the greatest players of all time.

The Dream Team scored at will. The rest of the world had to work just to get an open shot. In its eight Olympic contests, the U. S. won by an average of 43.8 points per game! In the medal round, the Dream Team whipped up on Lithuania, 127–76. In the finals, on August 8, 1992, the U. S. beat Croatia by 32, 117–85. The Croatians were led by three NBA players, Toni Kukoc, Dino Radja and Drazen Petrovic. But they were simply no match for the game's legends.

"The world's players eventually caught up with our best college players," said Daly. "And someday, possibly after we're all gone, they'll catch up with our best pros, too. When they do, we can all look back to 1992, when the Dream Team took the global game of basketball to a whole new level."

> "It was like coaching a bunch of rock stars," said Coach Chuck Daly.

SCOTTIE PIPPEN

Bull's-eye

Ask anyone who has ever met him. Michael Jordan is one of the most competitive people on Earth. He may deny it, but it's true. So when Michael returned to the NBA in 1995 after a short-lived baseball career, he had something to prove. And did he—and his Chicago Bulls—prove it!

Jordan had come back late in the 1994–95 season, but not in time to help his team win the title. With Michael at the helm, the Bulls had won championships in 1991, '92 and '93. So as the 1995–96 season opened, Michael and his teammates wanted to show the world that they were back. They won 10 of their first 12 games—and then they got hot!

At one point they reeled off an 18-game winning streak, one of the longest in league history. And then, after losing one, they went on another 13-game tear. They were almost unbeatable at home, taking their first 37 contests at the United Center. The Bulls were perfect hosts, right up until game time!

Even though every team in the league was gunning for them, the Bulls were almost always up to the task.

Coach Phil Jackson's team, already owners of three championship rings, were nearly as tough on the road. Even though every team in the league was gunning for them, the Bulls—Michael Jordan, Scottie Pippen, Dennis Rodman and their buddies—were almost always up to the task.

The NBA record for victories in a season was 69. It was owned by the 1971–72 Los Angeles Lakers (an earlier great moment), who won 33 in a row on their way to a 69–13 season. Early in the season, that became the Bulls' goal. And by midseason, they were well on their way. On February 2, 1996, Chicago was 41–3, an incredible .932 winning percentage.

Onward and upward went the Bulls, who kept their eye on the Laker mark. They caught L.A. in mid-April and had a chance to break it in Milwaukee on April 16. Traffic on the interstate highway from Chicago to Milwaukee was extra heavy that night. By game time, there were as many Bulls' fans as Bucks' supporters at the Bradley Center. Chicago didn't disappoint their fans, taking an 86–80 victory—their 70th—back to Illinois.

At season's end, the Bulls were 72–10, an unbelievable .878 winning percentage. Chicago was 39–2 at home and a league-record 31–8 on the road.

It was more of the same in the playoffs. The Bulls dispatched the Miami Heat, New York Knicks and Orlando Magic, losing only once. Then they took a 3–0 lead in the NBA Finals against Seattle before the Sonics won two straight at home. When the series returned to Chicago, however, the Bulls ended it quickly.

Overall, the Bulls won 87 of 100 games in their season-to-remember. And their fourth championship ring made it that much more memorable!

MICHAEL JORDAN

Michael's Last Shot

The greatest of all time? Name Michael Jordan and you're sure to get few arguments. And while Michael left a legacy of great shots, great defense and tremendous victories, he may well have saved his very best for last.

No one knew for sure, but M. J. had dropped plenty of hints that he would give it all up after the 1998 playoffs. His Chicago Bulls were seeking their sixth championship of the 1990s, something no team had accomplished since the Boston Celtics of the 1960s. That, said the so-called experts, would be enough for the incredibly competitive Michael.

Almost every NBA team has a "do-you-believe?" Michael story. But the Utah Jazz's tale of woe is among the most memorable.

The Bulls had a three games-to-two lead in the 1998 NBA Finals. Still, with the last two games scheduled for Salt Lake City's Delta Center, where the Jazz rarely lost, Utah could taste a title. In fact, with less than a minute to go in Game 6, Utah held a three-point lead.

He was dead tired.

Everyone was dead tired.

But Michael knew how to play through it.

That's when Michael took over. He scored on a typical M. J. drive to the basket, cutting the Jazz's lead to one. The layup marked Jordan's 42nd and 43rd points of the night. He was dead tired. Everyone was dead tired. But Michael knew how to play through it. "He had done it so often," said his teammate Steve Kerr. "We just jump on Michael's back and let him carry us."

Utah drove to the Chicago end. But Michael stripped the ball from Jazz star Karl Malone. "Utah tried to set a pick for Karl," said Jordan after the game. "But it didn't work. I was able to go back and knock the ball out of his hands. He never saw me coming."

Chicago ball, or more precisely, Jordan ball. The clock was ticking. Ten seconds to go, nine, eight. Instead of calling timeout, Jordan brought the ball up the court. There wasn't a question about what the Bulls were going to do. Everyone in the Delta Center knew, everyone watching on TV knew. And, of course, the Jazz knew.

Jordan drove to the hoop, but Utah's Bryon Russell blocked M. J.'s path to the bucket. So Michael stopped in his tracks, and Russell slipped and fell to the floor. Suddenly, Jordan had what basketball players call "a look." The clock continued to click away. Eight seconds, seven.

Given his "look," Michael Jordan never hesitated. Twenty feet from the basket, down one and with the game—maybe the championship—on the line, he fired.

The ball took what seemed like forever to reach its target. But when it got there, it was nothing but net. The Bulls led by one. The scoreboard read 87–86, Bulls. The clock read 5.2 seconds. All that was left was for Chicago to play defense. They did.

Michael's last NBA shot gave his Bulls their title. This, his final field goal, will be remembered forever.

DAVID ROBINSON
AND TIM DUNCAN

The Towers

There are all sorts of famous towers. There's the Eiffel Tower in Paris, the Leaning Tower in Pisa, and the legendary Tower of London. But in San Antonio, where the Alamo was once the most famous landmark, the Twin Towers reign instead.

When 7–0 Tim Duncan and 7–1 David Robinson led the San Antonio Spurs to the 1999 NBA championship, they took over ownership of the town, Alamo and all. Spurs fans had been hoping for a title ever since "Admiral" Robinson, the former Navy superstar, came to town in 1989. The Dream Teamer was everything he was advertised to be—scorer, rebounder, defender. The team had been a contender many times. But it could never reach the promised land—until Duncan came to Texas.

Duncan, a native of the U.S. Virgin Islands, came to basketball late. (Swimming was his favorite sport as a youngster.) But as soon as he got to Wake Forest University, everyone knew he was a serious player with the potential to be a superstar. The 1998–99 Spurs won 31 of their last 36 regular-season games, then went 15–2 in the playoffs. In fact, they wound up winning 15 of 17 playoff games, tying the all-time, four-round postseason record owned by the '89 Detroit Pistons and the '91 Chicago Bulls.

The Twin Towers were clearly the keys to the Spurs' success. For years, Robinson had been "the franchise." He was the focus of the offense. When Duncan arrived, things changed. The Admiral allowed the newcomer to take over the offense while he concentrated on defense. As a result, the Spurs became unstoppable—at both ends!

In the NBA Finals against the surprising New York Knicks, Duncan was dominant. With the Knicks' Patrick Ewing out with a leg injury, there was no one to guard Duncan. In the five games, Tim wrecked New York with 33, 25, 20, 28 and 31 points.

The Knicks, led by their swingman Latrell Sprewell (26 points per game) and guard Allan Houston (21.6 ppg), won Game 3 and kept the other four close. Sprewell scored a career play-off-high of 35 points in the final game, including 25 in the second half. In fact, it took 46 points and 19 rebounds from the Towers for San Antonio to win the final game, and it was close—78–77. The little guard, Avery Johnson, drained an 18-footer from the corner with 47 seconds left for the winning points. But it was the Spurs' defense, led by the 33-year-old Robinson, that held New York scoreless for the final three minutes and 12 seconds of the fourth quarter. That's what actually won the game.

"Tim Duncan is obviously the best player in the NBA," raved Knicks Coach Jeff Van Gundy when the series was over. "He's got great skills, of course. But it's his knowledge of the game and his incredible will to win that makes him great."

The Twin Towers were clearly the keys to the Spurs' success.